"Well, how did that make you feel?" Mom asks.
"Sad, because Aya is my friend and I don't like when she says sh" says quietly.
"It's okay that you weren't ready to share when Aya asked for the watercolors, but were you kind about saying no?" Mom asks.
"No...do you think she will stop being my friend?" Veer says, and he buries his face in his mom's lap.
"No, she will not stop being your friend," Mom says as she heads to the kitchen.
"Let's have some dessert, and you can tell me more."

Veer looks at the spread of his favorite desserts—kheer, gulab jamun, and rasmalai—on the table. As he continues telling his mom about his day, Baani suddenly starts crying. Mom turns away from Veer and picks Baani up. Veer jumps from the table and yells, "It's all her fault! She's always crying and taking you away!"

Veer's parents look at each other and give a silent nod.

Dad takes Baani to the bedroom while Mom scoops Veer into a tight hug. Tears stream down his face. "Oh, baby, I love you. I will always love you. I'm sorry. I know it's hard having a baby sister, but there will come a time when you will love her just like I love you." Veer sniffles into his mom.

"How about we have a special 'Veer and Mumma Day' this weekend? We can do anything you want...Anything! Then next weekend, we can have a 'Veer and Daddy Day.' What do you think?"

Veer's sniffles slowly come to a stop, and he says, "I liked it better when it was just you, me, and Daddy."

Mom's eyes well up. She pauses, takes a deep breath and says, "I know sharing is hard. Sharing me, Daddy, friends, watercolors, blocks—it can be tricky." But sometimes it's more fun to share than to have everything to yourself and have no one to share it with. "Like when you read a story with Baani, build a tall skyscraper with Henry, or paint a beautiful picture with Aya. It feels good to have a friend or a sister to play with.

Veer's First Day of School

For Mumma, Dad and Amrit

Written by Gursharan Bharth
Illustrated by Natalia Larguier

It was a crisp September, Monday morning. Veer was sitting on the floor building with his magna tiles. "Mom! Look how tall my tower is!" He said.

Veer's mom looked up and smiled as she packed his lunch for his first day of school.

She packed him some strawberries, cubes of cheese, a paratha, dahi, a juice box, and a chocolate chip cookie.

She paused to look over at Veer's structure and said, "Veer, that's a very tall tower! Good job baby!"

Veer's dad was tying his turban in front of the mirror. "Have a great day!" Mom yelled as both Veer and his mom grabbed their backpacks. "I love you Daddy! Veer added.

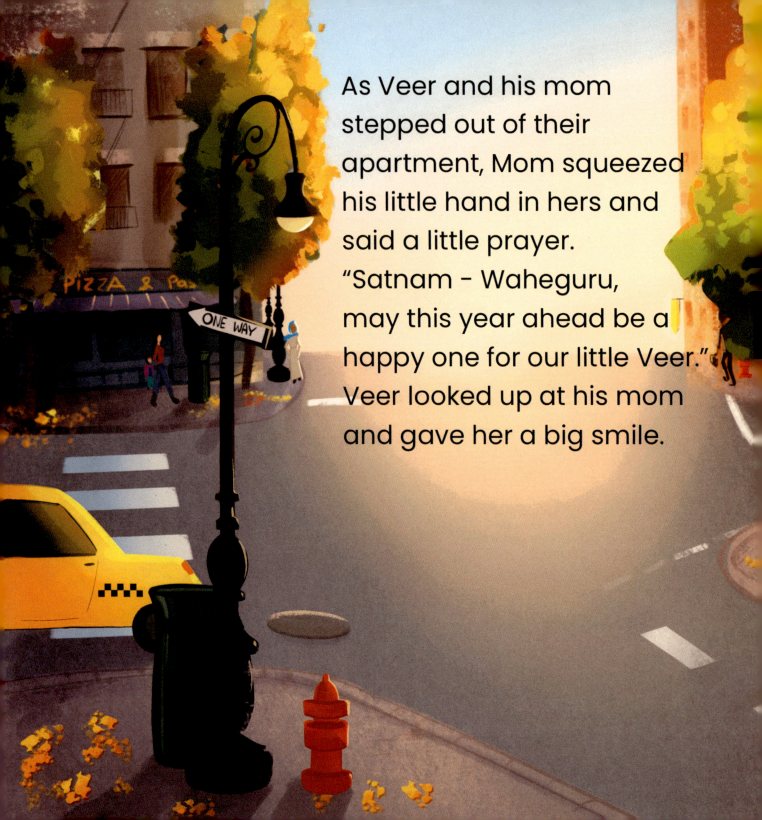

As Veer and his mom stepped out of their apartment, Mom squeezed his little hand in hers and said a little prayer.
"Satnam - Waheguru, may this year ahead be a happy one for our little Veer."
Veer looked up at his mom and gave her a big smile.

Veer and his mom walked to the subway. They hopped on to the 2 train to head downtown to Veer's new school.

When they arrived, Veer gave his mom a long tight hug...

... and took his teacher, Ms. Emmy's hand to walk to his new class.

During circle time, Veer introduced himself and sang the hello song with his classmates.

During play time, Veer spotted magna tiles and built a tower as tall as the one he had made at home. Aya and Jack, his classmates were also playing nearby.

It was finally lunch time. Veer's stomach was grumbling. He couldn't wait to eat his lunch! Veer got his lunchbox from his backpack and started unpacking his lunch.

He was sat at a table with Aya and Jack. He was still feeling pretty shy, so he quietly started eating his lunch.

Aya and Jack also took out their lunches and started eating too.

Aya had a sunflower butter and jelly sandwich, apples, and chocolate milk.

Jack had nuggets, a salad, and a chocolate chip cookie.

Veer broke off a piece of his paratha, dipped it into his dahi, and put it in his mouth. Aya looked at Veer's lunch curiously. "What are you eating?" She asked with a smile. Veer looked down at his lunchbox and said, "strawberries." "Oh, but what's the square bread, I've never seen that before." Jack chimed in. "It's a paratha, it's bread that my mommy made for me." Veer answered.

All three children finished their lunch, cleaned-up, and joined the line to go to the playground.

During recess, Veer, Aya, and Jack played freeze tag and chased each other around the playground. On their first day of school, Veer, Aya, and Jack were thrilled to have made new friends.

At the end of the day, Aya tapped Veer on his shoulder and said, "Tomorrow, I'm going to ask my daddy to pack me Meloui, that's the bread my mommy makes."

Veer smiled back at Aya and said, "I wonder what Meloui tastes like." "Maybe it tastes like Challah!" Jack added. Aya, Jack, and Veer's eyes grew big with wonder.

He waved goodbye to his two new friends, and ran to his parents.

Veer's mom and dad gave him a big hug and said, "You should feel so proud of yourself Veer! You had a great first day of school!"

20 Discussion Questions to Enhance Reading Comprehension

1. What was your favorite part of the book?

2. Who are the main characters in the book?

3. Where did the story take place?

4. What happened in the beginning, middle and end of the story?

5. How did Veer's feelings change from the beginning of the story to the end of the story?

6. Which part made you think of yourself?

7. Imagine you are Veer and it is your first day of school. How would you feel?

8. What do you think about the cover of this book?

9. Why do you think this book is called, Veer's First Day of School?

10. What is one thing you learned from reading this book?

11. What are some interesting words you saw in this book?

12. What do you know now that you did not know before you read this book?

13. What part of the book was the most like your home/school?

14. Which of the characters in this book is most like you? Why?

15. Which of the characters in this book is least like you? Why?

16. How do you make friends?

17. What is a good friend?

18. What can you say if you want to play with someone?

19. What is your favorite food?

20. What food is special in your home?

Book Extension Activities

- Nurture collaborative play skills by inviting your reader to engage in pretend play and act out the story or a part of the story.

- Build community by creating a classroom or home recipe book of special foods that classmates or family members love to eat.

- Strengthen cognitive, language and fine motor skills by making a paratha, or meloui or challah at school or at home!

- Foster empathy and perspective taking by inviting your reader to interview family members at home or peers at school about their favorite foods.

- Promote literacy skills by providing opportunities to retell the story using images from the story.

- Build language skills by creating a grocery list of all the items you need to create their favorite recipe.

- Boost cognitive, social-emotional, language, and academic skills by simply reading with your reader and inviting them to share their thoughts!

Draw a picture of your favorite school day lunch

What happened in the story?

FIRST

NEXT

THEN

AFTER

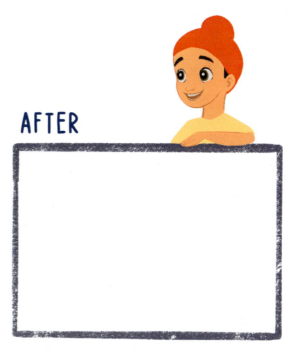

Mumma's Paratha Recipe

1. Add 2 cups of **atta** (whole wheat flour) and 1 cup of **pani** (water) into a shallow mixing bowl. Use your hands to knead the **atta**. Add additional **pani** as necessary to create soft and pliable dough.

2. Cover and let dough sit for 5 – 7 minutes.

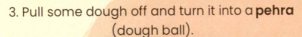

3. Pull some dough off and turn it into a **pehra** (dough ball).

4. Flatten and roll the **pehra** into a round flat circle called a **"roti."** Sprinkle flour as needed to keep the **pehra** from sticking to the surface.

5. Brush oil/butter and sprinkle **loon** (salt) & **mirch** (pepper) directly onto the surface of the roti.

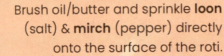

6. Fold 1/3 of the **roti** on both sides towards the center.